# BILLY AND THE MINI MONSTERS

## Monsters go Camping

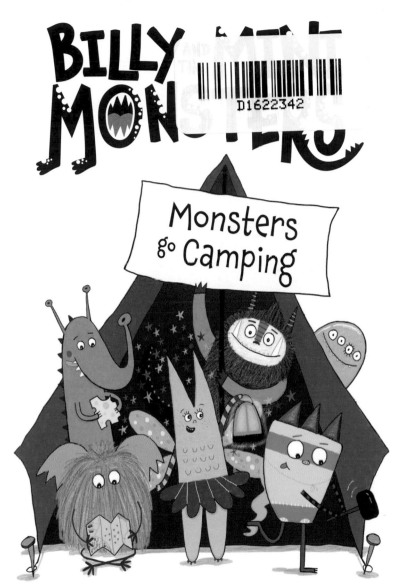

ZANNA DAVIDSON

Illustrated by MELANIE WILLIAMSON

## Meet Billy...

Billy was just
an ordinary boy
living an ordinary
life, until
**ONE NIGHT**
he found
five
**MINI
MONSTERS**
in his sock drawer.

Gloop   Peep   Fang-Face   Captain Snott   Trumpet

Then he saved their lives, and
they swore never to leave him.

We give you
the Secret-Hairy-
Snot-Tooth Oath
of Devotion.

When he
moved house,
Billy found
ANOTHER
monster.

Hello.
My name's
Sparkle-
Boogey.

One thing was certain – Billy's
life would never be the same AGAIN...

# Contents

# Chapter 1
# Werewolves and Bears

"I REALLY don't want to go on the school camping trip next weekend," said Billy.

"Why not?" asked his dad.

I used to love camping when I was your age.

"Remember how **WORRIED** I was about the **school diving competition?**" said Billy.

"And **when we moved**...

...and going on my first **school trip?**"

"Yes," said his dad. "And you got through them all!"

"Well, camping is the thing that makes me

## MOST WORRIED OF ALL.

I've even made a list."

# THINGS THAT MAKE ME SCARED OF GOING CAMPING:

Not being able to put up my tent →

Spiders getting into my tent

The dark OUTSIDE my tent

Having to go into the SCARY woods →

BEARS!!!

Needing to PEE in the night and having to find the TOILET IN THE DARK

Getting lost IN THE DARK on my way to the TOILET

WEREWOLVES (everyone says they're not real but what if they are?)

"Billy," said his dad. "There are **NO** bears where you're going. You'll be with your class AND you're sharing a tent with your best friend."

What's more, werewolves **DEFINITELY** don't exist.

"I have to take your sister to her kung fu class now. We can talk about this again later."

And he left.
Billy sat on his bed, feeling glum.
One by one, his Mini Monsters
peered out from his sock drawer.

We'll come and look after you, Billy.

You're the best!

Billy showed them the camping booklet he'd been given.

"Here's a map of the campsite," he said.

Billy and Ash, your tent is here

Site 10

Site 9

STREAM

Site 8

Site 6

CAMPING AREA

Site 5

Site 2

CAMPFIRE

BOATING LAKE

WOODS

Site 7

Site 4

Site 3

Site 1

TOILETS

SHOWERS

# "And the school sent us this as well..."

<u>Plan for the Camping Trip</u>

<u>Saturday afternoon</u>

3 p.m. Take bus from school to campsite.

What if I feel sick on the bus?

4 p.m. Bus arrives at parking lot. One-mile walk to campsite.

ONE MILE! That's SO far!

5 p.m. Put up tents.

Argh!!! How?? Tents are IMPOSSIBLE.

6 p.m. Dinner & marshmallows around the campfire.

Hooray! A fun part!

7 p.m. Go to sleep.

There's **NO WAY** I'm going to sleep.

I'm going to stay up to watch out for WEREWOLVES.

"It's basically two days of DOOM," said Billy.

Sunday morning

8 a.m. Breakfast.

Choc milk

Yum!

9 a.m. Camping competition in the woods.

I'm sure I will FAIL.

12 a.m. Bus returns to school.

1 p.m. Parents to pick up students from school gates.

Unless I've been devoured by werewolves/bears/an army of ants/gotten lost in the woods forever...

Billy sighed as he looked at the Mini Monsters. "I don't even know **HOW** to put up a tent. And the toilets are about a **MILLION** miles away!"

What happens if there's a bear **LURKING** by the toilets?

I can fight a bear! I'll just shoot out jets of glitter.

And I'll scare away the spiders with my **TERRIFYING** fangs.

I can **GLOW** in the dark, so you don't have to be scared at night.

I'll use my cheese-powered **TOOTS** to fend off a werewolf.

"So you see," said Gloop, patting Billy's hand. "There's nothing to be worried about."

"What about you, Peep?" asked Billy. "I know you get anxious too."

"Hmm," said Peep, fluttering his wings. "How long until the camping trip?"

"A week," said Billy.

Peep smiled. "I have a plan!"

Always be prepared...

The next day - Saturday:
Learn how to place sticks for a fire.
(Do not light without a grown-up.)

21

**Tuesday: Practice putting up a tent in under a minute.**

Ready, set... GO!

Ta da!

Good job, Peep. You did that in fifty seconds.

Hmm.

**Wednesday: Make sure you can map read.**

**Thursday: Learn how to tie a knot.**

**Friday: Monsters are prepared!**

Now we can camp with confidence!

23

## Chapter 2
# To the Campsite

On the day of the camping trip, Billy's dad dropped him off at school. Billy lined up behind Ms. Potts, the teacher.

Please say "here" when I call your name. Keira, Billy, Ash, Madhura...

Billy took a quick peek inside his backpack to check on the Mini Monsters.

All okay?

Yes, Billy!

Then he sat down on the bus, next to his best friend, Ash.

"Isn't this great?" said Ash.

But even with the Mini Monsters, Billy still felt really nervous.

He couldn't even join in when everyone on the bus started singing camping songs.

"You're **SCARED**, aren't you?" said Jack, who was sitting in front of them.

"**Raaaaar!**" said Jack's friend, Sam, making a werewolf face.

"Ignore them," said Ash.
"Camping is going to be

# AWESOME!

There'll be…"

Billy was just starting to feel better when Ash said, "And, best of all, we'll be sleeping in the

# WOODS AT NIGHT!"

Suddenly, all Billy could think about were lots of eyes, watching him from the darkness…

…AND A

BEAR

CREEPING UP ON HIM…

ARGH!

By the time they arrived, Billy had a tight, knotted feeling in his tummy.

"Okay, everyone," said Ms. Potts. "It's a thirty minute walk from here to the campsite. Follow me!"

You can do this, Billy!

"Maybe everything will be okay," thought Billy. "Maybe camping will be fun after all."

Then his boot got stuck.

"Don't worry," said Ash. "I'll get you out. One, two, three…"

"Yes, this is definitely

# THE WORST DAY OF MY LIFE,"

thought Billy. "And I still have
the night to get through."

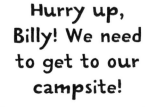

Hurry up,
Billy! We need
to get to our
campsite!

By the lake...

Oh no, we've lost Billy!

That's not a problem! I have a map of the campsite.

Always be prepared!

This is where we need to get to.

34

36

37

# Chapter 3
# The Toilet of Doom

By the time they arrived at the campsite, Billy was very cold and very wet and very muddy.

Site 9

"Don't worry, Billy," said Ash. "We'll soon have our tent up."

"I know," thought Billy. "I'll ask Peep. He's the camping expert." But when Billy looked in his backpack he realized that the

# Mini Monsters were GONE!

"Where could they be?" wondered Billy.

Back on the bus?

Lost on the walk?

Captured by BEARS?

Before Billy could work out a plan, one of the teachers came over.

"What's going on here?" said Mr. Gritton. "This tent is a mess! I think... yes... you've put it up INSIDE OUT."

"Go and join the others by the campfire," sighed Mr. Gritton. "I'll sort this out..."

"Yum!
Marshmallows!"
said Ash.
Unfortunately,
Billy set fire to his.
By the time they were back in
their tent, it was already dark.
And Billy still hadn't had a chance
to look for his monsters.

Let's tell
each other
spooky stories!

Um, no
thanks!

A moment later, Ash was fast asleep and snoring. Billy lay awake in the dark.

"How am I going to find the monsters?" he thought. "Oh no. Even worse…"

I NEED TO PEE!

There was only one thing to do. He was going to have to visit

# THE TOILET OF DOOM.

45

46

47

# Chapter 4
# Lost in the Woods

Billy had found the toilet. He was feeling extremely proud of himself.

I did it! I walked to the toilet **ON MY OWN**, in the **DARK!**

TOILET

"Maybe this camping thing isn't so bad after all," thought Billy. "Maybe I've got what it takes to be a FAMOUS EXPLORER."

Then his light **WENT OUT**.

"I don't want to be an explorer," thought Billy. "I NEVER want to go camping again. I can't even see where my tent is."

Billy started walking. "I think it's this way," he said to himself. "Although I don't remember it taking so long…"

It was then he started to hear noises. Tiny little noises. And there was a little glowing light, coming towards him.

Is it an alien?

A one-eyed werewolf?

The next thing Billy knew, something slimy was brushing against his leg.

There was
something
in his
hair too...

...and wings,
fluttering
against
his face.

# BILLY SCREAMED!

At that moment, the moon came out from behind a cloud and Billy saw them...

Don't be scared.

It's us!

Together, they walked back to the
tent, Captain Snott lighting the way.
"Oh!" said Billy, when they got
back. "I was never very far away."

Ash was still **snoring** as Billy climbed into his sleeping bag. "I faced my worst fear tonight," he whispered sleepily, "and I was fine."

"Maybe," Billy went on, with a final yawn, "I'll be a great explorer after all..."

56

In Jack's tent...

Argh!

UFO

Mmm. These look tasty.

Oops!

59

# Chapter 5
# Camping Champion

Billy woke to a bright, sunny morning. The Mini Monsters were lying next to him, tucked up in their little sock sleeping bags.

"Morning, Ash!" said Billy, as Ash opened his eyes. "Isn't it a beautiful day!"

But outside the tent, the other kids were looking **SCARED** and **ALARMED**.

I saw something **GLOWING** in the night.

Something came and tickled my feet!

Pitch 9

Afterwards, Ms. Potts gathered everyone together.

"We're going to do a competition in the woods," she said. "I'll divide you into teams: Jack, Yasmin, Sam, Ash and Billy are on one team. Who wants to be team leader?"

"Here's what you have to do," said Ms. Potts, handing them a sheet of paper. "Good luck."

"**Follow me!**" Billy told his team.

"**This will be great.**"

But there might be werewolves in there.

There's nothing to be afraid of. Trust me!

Billy and his team made a shelter..

...followed a trail...

Stream

...tied a knot...

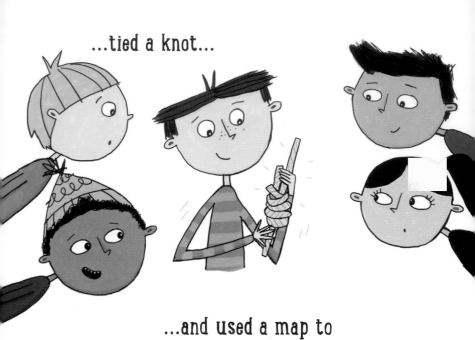

...and used a map to find some treasure.

"Congratulations!" said Ms. Potts. "Your team has won the camping competition."

Jack turned to Billy. "Nice work, Billy," he said. "Sorry we teased you before. You led us through the scary woods."

You're the **CAMPING CHAMPION!**

69

The mountains?

The desert?

The jungle?

70

# Chapter 6
# Under the Stars

When Billy stepped off the school bus, his dad was there to collect him and Ash.

"How was the trip?" asked
Billy's dad, as they walked home.
"It was AMAZING!" said Billy.

Billy was a camping champion!

"It was great because you were
there to help me," Billy told Ash.
Ash grinned, before running down
the sidewalk to his house. "See you
at school on Monday," he said.

73

"Actually," said Billy, turning to his dad, "can we all camp in the backyard tonight? I think I feel brave enough."

"Of course," said his dad. "You and Ruby can camp out first, and then your mom and I will join you later."

Ruby fell asleep almost immediately, but Billy and his Mini Monsters sat out together, looking up at the stars.

When they were finally ready for sleep, they crawled into the tent and snuggled down in their sleeping bags.

"Good night, Mini Monsters," said Billy.

"Good night, Billy," they replied.

"This is PERFECT," said Billy.
Then came a small TOOT!
followed by a TERRIBLE smell.
"Trumpet!" they all cried.

Even with Trumpet's toot, Billy
looked around the tent and smiled.
He really loved camping!

# All about the MINI MONSTERS

## CAPTAIN SNOTT →

LIKES EATING: boogeys.

SPECIAL SKILL:
can glow in the dark.

SCARE
FACTOR:
5/10

SCARE
FACTOR:
4/10

## ← GLOOP

LIKES EATING: cake.

SPECIAL SKILL:
very stre-e-e-e-tchy.
Gloop can also swallow his own
eyeballs and make them reappear
on any part of his body.

## FANG-FACE →

LIKES EATING:
socks, school ties, paper, or
anything that comes his way.

SPECIAL SKILL:
has massive fangs.

SCARE
FACTOR:
9/10

# TRUMPET →

LIKES EATING: cheese.

SPECIAL SKILL:
amazingly powerful
cheese-powered toots.

**SCARE FACTOR:**
**7/10**
(taking into
account his toots)

# PEEP

LIKES EATING: very small flies.

SPECIAL SKILL: can fly (but
not very far, or very well).

**SCARE FACTOR:**
**0/10** (unless you're afraid of
small hairy things)

# SPARKLE-BOOGEY

LIKES EATING:
glitter and boogeys.

SPECIAL SKILL:
can shoot out
clouds of glitter.

**SCARE FACTOR:**
**5/10** (if you're scared of
pink sparkly glitter)

Series editor: Becky Walker
Designed by Brenda Cole
Cover design by Hannah Cobley
Reading consultant: Alison Kelly
American editor: Carrie Armstrong

This edition first published in 2020 by Usborne Publishing Ltd.,
Usborne House, 83-85 Saffron Hill, London EC1N 8RT, England.
usborne.com © 2020, 2021 Usborne Publishing Ltd. The name Usborne
and the Balloon logo are Trade Marks of Usborne Publishing Ltd.
All rights reserved. No part of this publication may be reproduced,
stored in a retrieval system or transmitted in any form or by any
means, electronic, mechanical, photocopying, recording or otherwise
without the prior permission of the publisher. UE. This edition
first published in America 2021. EDC, Tulsa, Oklahoma 74146
usbornebooksandmore.com